Jared,
You are a littl[e]
stinky and naiv[e]
I love you! Thanks
always supporting my id[eas]
ideas. Truly I think you ...

[signature]

Second *Love* in New York City

Keri Brooks McWhorter

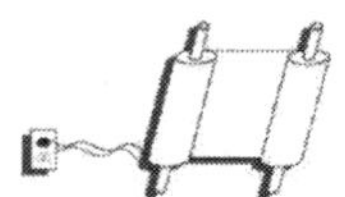

Cover Design by Steven Novak of Novak Illustrations.

Interior design by M. Borgnaes of The Electric Scroll.

Dedication

To my Dad who will cringe knowing his name is on the pages of a romance book, but has constantly encouraged me to put my talent on paper. Thanks for passing down your imagination and ADHD to me.

Chapter One

I can't believe Angela talked me into this. I paced behind my front door, looking out the peep hole, then the window. Maybe this was my sister's early Christmas gift to me. One that I wanted to return. My flats tapped on the tile floor with each step. What if I say something stupid? What if I end up with food in my teeth or snort when I laugh? If I laugh at all.

"Ugh!"

This is such a waste of time. Is it too late to cancel? I know Angela meant well but she knows how I feel about dating and marriage, so how did she talk me into a date? A blind date nonetheless.

I heard a knock at the door. I must have missed him walking up the steps while I was shaking my fists at the ceiling and feeling sorry for myself. I took a deep breath and opened the door.

"Hi," I muttered. I sounded like I was ten years old and this was my first encounter with the opposite sex.

"Hello, I'm Sam." He smiled.

"I'm Madelyn, nice to meet you." I put my hand out to shake his, realizing too late I should have kept my hands to my side. He gave me an awkward smile and took my hand to give me a weak, clammy shake. I gulped in disgust and whisked my hand away quickly. The fact that I rarely date had become obvious at that moment.

"You ready to go?" he asked cheerfully, wiping his sweaty hand on his pants.

"Yes," I muttered. I couldn't quite get my words out, but no, I wasn't ready for this. I rubbed my hands across my pants too. I tried to remember if I had some hand sanitizer in my purse.

I think I'll stop answering the phone altogether after this. Is it possible to know within seconds of meeting someone if you like them or not? Because I already knew.

He was probably a foot shorter than me, with blonde hair; at least what was left of it. A possible comb-over? I wasn't sure what was going on there. I felt like I was staring at a live mugshot, or maybe a neighborhood peeping tom.

"You okay?" he asked. His eyes squinted as we walked to the car.

I had been staring at him and quite possibly making some sort of disgusted-confused combination face. I quickly shook my face into a smile. "I'm good. Just a little nervous, I guess."

"Your sister mentioned that you haven't been on a date in a year or so."

I just smiled and shook my head. *Wow, thanks Angela. What else did she tell you?*

I was surprised when we pulled into Chick-Fil-A. I admit I love the place, but I had a different setting in my head. He picked a table in the middle of all the action. Kids yelled and jumped up and down in their seats while their parents ignored their antics.

A man dressed as a cow stood near the order line with balloons strung up behind him. The door to the play center opened and shut, allowing laughter to go in and out of ear shot. It was a good distraction for me.

"What would you like?" he asked, interrupting my thoughts once again.

"I love their cobb salad." I tried to smile.

"Oh, I thought maybe you'd like a sandwich," he said slowly.

My eyes squinted in confusion.

"You know, their regular Chick-Fil-A sandwich." He shook and tilted his head to the side as if to remind me that that is what I wanted.

"That sounds great." I didn't even try to smile this time.

When it was his turn to order, I watched him hand over a coupon for a free sandwich. I hid my face in my hands. *This is not happening.*

When he returned, I quickly ate my sandwich and the few fries that he set between us to share.

"You eat fast," he said, throwing his head back with laughter. But this was not an ordinary laugh. It sounded like a horse. A drunk horse.

"Glad my eating amuses you," I said. I didn't see how Angela could have ever thought Sam would be a good match for me. What was she trying to do?

"So, what is it exactly that you do for a living?" he changed the subject as his chuckle came to a halt.

I looked up to answer him and there it was, a piece of lettuce stuck between his two front teeth. I didn't know if I could continue on with the night. I closed my eyes and prayed him gone, but when I opened them he was still there.

"I work at a counseling center for troubled kids and teens," I disclosed with a slight sigh. I didn't want him to know anything about me.

"Oh, did you end up there after your husband died?" he asked solemnly, still with green in his teeth.

I exhaled deeply. I usually didn't mind talking about it. But tonight, coming from his mouth, I was almost offended. "Yes," was all I could muster.

"Your sister told me you were an accountant until Luke died and then—"

"I'm feeling sick to my stomach. I think it was the sandwich. Please excuse me." I quickly shot up from the table and headed for the bathroom.

"It couldn't have been the sandwich," he mumbled as I walked away. I locked myself in the largest stall and started pacing. I pulled out my phone and started texting. The first one to Angela, cursing her and her awfulness. Then one to Ben.

Help me please. EMERGENCY!!

He quickly texted back.

What happened? Are you ok? Do you need me to come and get you?

Major date fail. I don't know what to do. He just brought up Luke and I can't take it.

Ok, calm down, you are going to be fine. Go back out there, tell him you don't feel well and ask him to take you

home.

It was a plan I could have and should have easily come up with on my own, but for some reason, I needed to hear it from Ben.

Sam wasn't happy when I shared the news with him. "What about the rest of our date? We were going to take a walk in downtown Gilbert and look at the Christmas lights. And then I have coupons…I mean, I wanted to get you a Frosty at Wendy's."

After about five minutes of trying to explain my fake illness to him he conceded and agreed to leave, but not before he asked the cashier for a refund on the sandwich that made his date sick. The free sandwich. What a tight-wad. Finally, after what seemed liked hours, we walked outside into the Arizona winter. I could breathe again. I buttoned up my light coat, wrapped a scarf around my neck, opened my own car door and shut it behind me before Sam could get there.

"Is Ben the reason why you don't usually date?" Sam asked after a beautifully silent five-minute drive.

My eyes widened and my fists tightened in my lap. "Ben and I are best friends, Sam, and I rarely date because I don't want to be married again. Ever. It's that simple," I said, looking directly at him.

We pulled up to my house and he put the car in park. "I had a lovely time Maddie. Can I call you Maddie?"

That was it, I couldn't take it anymore!

"I can't do this." I blurted directly to Sam. "Thanks for the sandwich, I think you are a nice guy, just not the guy for me. Please don't call me again." I exited the car as fast as I could.

"Wait!" he yelled stumbling out of his side of the car, "I

bought you French fries and I was going to get you ice cream, too." He now had his own hands up in the air, "Your sister said you were—"

I slammed my front door behind me before I could hear what else my sister said. I locked the door and laid my head back against it, taking in a deep breath. *Does Angela even know me at all?*

Chapter Two

All I wanted to do was put on my pajamas, break open a Dove Bar, and catch up on *Greys Anatomy*. I plugged in the lights to my Christmas tree, smelling the pine needles as they brushed my face.

I plopped down on my couch and Bucket jumped into my lap. I had always been obsessed with English Bulldogs and finally gave in to buying one after my husband died. He was loyal, kind, and very cuddly. I pulled him in close to me and stroked his back while I snatched the remote and located my show.

I grabbed my phone, turning the sound back on. There were a million text messages from Angela. *Erase. Erase. Erase*. Then one from Melanie.

How did the date go, Mom?

She was still hoping some man might catch my eye.

She was getting married in a week and somehow during all her planning she still had time for my love life. She texted again.

Don't forget to finish packing, I don't want to miss the plane tomorrow.

I had mostly everything packed. It would not only be my first Christmas away from Arizona but my first time in New York City. I started to text Mellie back when my phone beeped again.

It was Ben.

Did he kiss you? Did you fall in love and run off to Vegas?

No, I did not kiss, fall in love, or go to Vegas.

Oh good cuz I still need you to pick up my tux in the morning.

Oh ha ha thanks for caring.

I do care. Care that my tux is taken care of.

I changed the subject.

Do you want to come over and watch Seinfeld or something? I have extra chocolate, or I'm sure I can muster up the energy to cook you up a cheeseburger or something.

Can't. Heather is here right now.

I always got a little sad when he mentioned Heather. *The other woman* is what I privately referred to her as. Ben's girlfriend of almost seven months. She was sweet and beautiful and very eager to marry.

She is there right now with you and you are texting me? What is wrong with you?

It's fine, I just took a quick break to check on my best friend.

Ok fine, call me tomorrow then.

I liked Heather, but sometimes I wanted Ben all to myself.

I heard giggling as Mellie and Jared walked through the front door. I smiled thinking about the great man she found to marry. Even though they'd known each other for years, they say they fell in love in New York City. They spent a semester there through a college history course.

"Hi, Mom." Mellie smiled, still holding Jared's hand.

"Hey, Mom; heard your date went well." Jared laughed.

I loved that he called me Mom.

"My Dad wanted me to remind you to get his tux in the morning."

I laughed. "He just texted me about it." I rolled my eyes. "He has Heather over there and he is bossing me around over here."

My encounters with Heather have always been short, so my already anxious self was worried about what a trip will be like with her tagging along.

Chapter Three

The next morning, Mellie came over to help me finish packing.

"Mom, can you fit both dresses in here?" Mellie asked.

"I think so; let me see."

"Oh, and don't forget your slip and your big coat." Mellie continued.

"What time is Jared picking us up?" I asked.

We'd had to go out and find heavy winter coats to take to New York. They weren't a usual thing to find in my Arizona closet. I'd tried to talk Mellie into a spring wedding, but they didn't want to wait. I didn't blame them.

"Uhm, in about 20 minutes; we have to hurry. Oh, and Mom did you pack *both* of those dresses I bought for you?"

I gave Mellie a little smirk. She is very stylish and thinks I should dress sexier than I do. So, for her wedding, she bought me two dresses. One that is conservative and fits the mom-of-the-bride stereotype and another dress that said something else. Although I'm not quite sure what. I said I would bring it but made no promises to wear it. I think she's still hoping, though.

"I packed them," I said. "It's beautiful Mellie, but a little too fancy and sexy for me don't you think?"

She just smiled and walked off.

I set my bags at the front door and as I turned around, Mellie stood directly in front of me and put her hands on my shoulders. "Mom, listen; Heather is coming." She sounded serious.

"I know; it's fine," I said quickly, breaking her hold and turning to look out the window.

"No, listen." There was a short pause. "You know I don't really like her but whatever; I'll get over it. It's you I'm worried about."

"Mellie, I'm…."

I tried to speak, but Mellie interrupted me, putting both hands back on my shoulders and looking intently into my eyes.

"You've never been around the two of them together for a long period of time. It will be kind of awkward. You won't have your Benny like you're used to."

"I'll be fine. I'm a grown woman. Maybe she's meant to be his wife and I need to get used to her," I said, but I wasn't sure if I quite believed it.

"No, Mom, you don't mean that. You should be his wife. Ben loves *you*," Mellie said. She took her hands off my shoulders and looked out the window for Jared.

"Mellie, we've talked about this a million times. I've had my one true love and I want to hold on to that forever." I tilted my head smiling as if it was both a scolding and a declaration.

"Mom, it's okay to love someone else. Dad wants you to be happy; he wants *us* to be happy."

I quickly imagined Luke's face. Blonde hair, blue eyes, with a big smile, always.

"He's been gone three years now Mom. If you gave Ben a chance, it would just mean that your love would grow. That's all."

Luke's face disappeared, and I saw Ben, my now best friend, whose face looked very different. I was back to reality.

"Oh Mellie." I could see her eyes begin to water. I grabbed her and hugged her close. I kissed her forehead. "My sweet girl." I pulled her back to face me, wiping her tears from her eyes. It makes me feel so good to be needed like this still. "I'm happy; as happy as I can be without your Dad here. You know that." I wiped my now streaming tears on the bottom of my sleeve.

She stepped back and wiped a tear from her face. "I know you're happy. I just see Ben all the time and think that you could make him happy, too. The way he talks about you, Mom, and the way he looks at you, how could you not—"

The doorbell rang and saved me from having to talk about it further. Again. It's a conversation many have tried to have with me; everyone except Ben.

Caroline, Ben's youngest daughter, was at the door. She flung it the rest of the way open and an old memory flashed through my mind of the first time I ever met her beautiful mother Cassie.

> *It was ten years ago. We had just moved in and she came over to meet us with a plate of chocolate chip cookies. I didn't hear the door*

bell and when I swung the front door open to grab more boxes from the moving truck, there she was with a big, friendly smile. We were good friends from then on.

My heart skipped a beat seeing Caroline standing there with the same smile. She was eighteen and just three years younger than Jared and Mellie; Ben's only other child, aside from Jared.

Spunky, fun, loyal, and little rebellious; I loved that about her. She spent a lot of time at our house these past couple of years since her mother passed. Mellie and I kind of took her under our wing and just loved her. She hugged me strongly. Ben and Jared followed Caroline up the walk to get our bags.

"Let me get that, Mellie, you just hop in the shuttle," Jared said as he greeted his fiancé with a kiss.

He's so good to her. Kind-hearted and strong; loving, hardworking, and very handsome, just like his father. I feel like I knew years ago that the two of them would end up together. Of course, Mellie doesn't like it if I tell her that. But it's true. He was constantly over here, too, sometimes without Caroline. He always smiled at Mellie even when she wasn't looking.

Caroline locked arms with mine as we walked down the path to the van. "Please sit next to me; please," she begged. "I can't stand Heather's fake smile, and fake laugh, and ridiculous stories." She rolled her eyes.

I laughed and promised I would. For the last few months, I've heard Caroline go on and on about how much she disliked Heather, listing among her unappealing attributes that she laughs like a donkey braying: she is way too nice; and she invades personal space.

Sometimes when Heather was over at their house, Caroline would come and stay with us until she went home. I think she's hated any woman her dad has dated after her mom died. I found Heather to be very nice during my short encounters with her. I still wanted to hate her.

Caroline was pretty open about not liking her, especially her laugh. Maybe Heather the donkey-brayer and Sam the horse-laugher would make a better match.

The shuttle ride to the airport was not too long, but everyone had coupled off into their own conversations.

Jared and Mellie talked about wedding stuff and held each other close, kissing between thoughts.

Caroline stuck her earbuds in and looped her arm in mine while laying her head on my shoulder.

I laid my head back and closed my eyes for a moment. My thoughts quickly jumped back to mine and Mellie's conversation, especially when she said that I 'could make him happy too'. Was Ben unhappy? He seemed pretty happy to me.

I opened my eyes, leaning forward just a little to observe Heather and Ben for a while. She was, indeed, a close talker, stroking his face and arm while talking and talking. It did feel a bit strange to see him with her. I could understand a little better what Caroline meant.

She was pretty; shoulder-length blonde hair with green eyes, nice figure. She was maybe a few inches shorter than me. I'd been on a few group dates with Ben when he was with other women. I'd never seen him flirt with them or show romantic interest in them. He seemed very interested in Heather.

* * * * *

The airplane was packed. I started to get nervous as soon as I boarded.

Ben put his hand on my shoulder. "Will you be all right?" he said softly. He knows my fear of flying.

"Yes, thank you. I brought something to calm my nerves," I said confidently. Which reminded me; I'd forgotten to take it ahead of time. As soon as I sat down I searched through my purse. "Where did I put it?" I whispered to myself. I was five seats in front of Ben and Heather and directly behind Jared, Caroline, and Mellie. I couldn't find the pills. Ben must have sensed my frustration and texted me.

Are you ok, what are you doing? You look like a crazy woman!

I might be a crazy woman, I can't find my anti-crazy pills!

A few minutes later Heather showed up by my side and unfolded her hand down close to my face then leaned in, a little too close. "Here, this will help." She smiled.

"What is it?" I asked.

"Don't worry about it, just take it, I promise it will take the edge off and you will have a great flight."

Just so she would back away, I took it out of her hand, staring at its odd shape.

Mellie turned around in her seat. "Take it, Mom; you deserve a stress-free airplane ride. Just relax." She smiled. She understands more than anyone how much I hate to fly. Well, her and Ben.

Our families flew to California a year ago to visit the

beach. Ben sat next to me on the plane and at some point, he had taken my hand and held it almost the whole way there. I wished he was sitting next to me right now.

I took the pill and shortly thereafter fell asleep. My phone buzzed in my lap startling me awake. I forgot to turn it off. It was Ben. Who shouldn't have his phone on either.

You ok?

I thought about it and realized that I was more than okay. I felt great. Maybe Heather wasn't so bad after all, trying to help me out. I felt like I could jump out of this airplane and fly to wherever I wanted to go. I smiled thinking about flying and then realized I really had to pee.

I texted Ben back.

I feel great, honestly, I just have to pee really bad.

Why do you feel the need to tell me that?

I didn't need to tell him that, but it had made sense in the moment. I stood up a little too fast and everything spun just a little. I patted the heads of Mellie, Caroline and Jared. They all turned around and gave me questionable smiles.

I walked past Ben and Heather slowly, smiling, I think. I bent down to be closer to them. "You two really are cute together; you know that?" I said, almost a little too loud. Heather belted out her donkey laugh, and Ben flashed me a concerned smile.

I kept walking past them toward the bathroom and found it quite difficult to reach my destination. I felt Ben grab onto my elbow speaking quietly. "Here, let me help you," he said.

"Oh, Benny, why are you always so good to me?" I tried to speak quietly, but it kept coming out louder than I anticipated. It felt like the longest journey to get to the back of the plane. I then realized there was a closer bathroom to my seat at the front of the plane. How did I miss that?

Ben opened the door for me and asked if I could manage from here. I chuckled at the thought of him helping me in the bathroom. I turned to him and patted his cheek, lightly scratching the dark stubble on his face with my nails. He was still holding my arms to keep me somewhat steady.

"Oh Benny, you are so handsome, so very handsome." I said quietly. I ran my fingers through his dark hair.

His brown eyes grew big, unsure of how to respond. I kept talking. "You know that was a good kiss between us in California." His eyes widened even more, and he grew uncomfortable. "You remember, Benny? That night on the pier? You are an exceptional kisser." My body swayed to the left as I tried to keep my eyes on Ben.

"I remember," he said quickly. "Are you ok? You look pale."

I didn't feel well, as a matter of fact. I just realized it in the moment he said it. I quickly turned and found myself puking in the tiny airplane toilet.

It wasn't quiet puking; rather a very loud, repetitive barfing. I could feel Ben behind me rubbing my back and holding my messy, dark-blonde hair up with his other hand. I was so glad he was there but also mortified at the same time. I went into dry heaving and after it slowed, I asked Ben to leave so I could close the door and collect myself.

After about twenty minutes, I felt well enough to go back to my seat. Many of the passengers were staring at me in disgust. I forced a smile on my face. "Don't eat the chicken," I said. No one laughed at me.

I slowly walked back to my seat, passing Heather and Ben. She had fallen asleep and Ben started to get up, looking concerned. I motioned for him to sit down and whispered, "I'm fine."

I walked slowly to my seat and rested my head back. I fell asleep quickly and when I woke, I felt like someone had hit me over the head with a frying pan. The back of my eyes pounded. I put on a pair of sunglasses to try and decrease the pain from the light. I only remember a few details after that. Waiting for luggage and feeling queasy, boarding a taxi with a guy named Chad and then Mellie helping me into my hotel bed.

Chapter Four

I woke up the next morning feeling much better. Great in fact. I took a deep breath and stretched my arms and legs. I snuggled back into the soft hotel pillows. I thought about this wonderful trip to New York and Mellie marrying a wonderful man and then I remembered.

I remembered everything. I sat up in bed and tried to piece together the events that had unfolded on the airplane. *What did Heather give me?* I thought. *Did she mean to make me feel that way?* Oh, the headache and the puking and Benny holding my hair! Benny....

"Oh, my goodness." I laid back in bed. I realized what I had done. "No, No, no!" I shook my head and hid my face in my hands. Did I really run my fingers through his hair and talk about our kiss? Our kiss!

About a year ago we decided it would be fun for our families to take a vacation together. We flew together on the same flight and got hotel rooms right next to each other. We did everything together that weekend; surfing at the beach, shopping, eating out, and Universal Studios. On the last night Jared, Caroline, and Melanie planned a date for the two of us to be alone. I should have known they were up to something. They always made it so that Ben and I were sitting together; on the plane, in the car, at restaurants, and on all the rides. We decided to go but I made it clear it would only be as friends. They had reservations for us at a nice restaurant, Café Sierra, and recommended a walk down the beach and pier afterward.

"Are you cold?" Ben asked as we got close to the end of the pier. "Yes, a little." He took his coat off and wrapped it around me. We reached the end of the pier and set our arms on the railing.

"Our kids are so sweet, trying to set us up on a date," I said, laughing a little.

"Yes, they're good kids." He smiled. Ben wouldn't look at me, he seemed uncomfortable gazing at the black expanse of sea beyond the pier.

"Are you nervous?" I asked with a smile.

"No, just not quite used to this weather," he said without conviction. We listened to the waves crashing in and I felt Ben move closer to me. It felt comfortable and warm, reminding me of my Luke. Ben turned his body toward me. I blurted

my thoughts, "Luke would have loved this, he always loved going to the beach, surfing, the sun. Cassie would have loved it, too, I think. Did she like the ocean?"

He looked at me for a second, then turned his body back to face the ocean. "She would have loved to just be here with her family, but she was a lake person; boating, water skiing, and a fire pit out by the lake to cook up the fish we caught for the day." He smiled thinking about her, I knew he absolutely loved her. We stood in silence for a while, thinking about our loved ones who were now gone.

"I miss kissing." I interrupted the quiet.

"What?" Ben said with a surprised laugh.

"Kissing; I miss kissing and holding hands and cuddling and.... You know, being close to someone," I replied almost sadly.

"Yes, I know," he said. We again looked out toward the water. "Friends could kiss sometimes," he turned and smiled at me.

I laughed.

"Yeah, well why not?" he continued.

"Like friends can listen to 'Endless Love' in the dark." I laughed at myself.

His head flew back in laughter. I loved making him laugh. We chuckled for a while and then silence came only to be interrupted by a few straggling laughs from the both of us.

"Okay," I finally blurted out.

"Okay, you're ready to head back?" Ben

said as he took his hands off the railing.

"Okay, let's kiss," I said uncertainly. I had not wanted to kiss anyone since Luke died, but that night felt different. Maybe it was the beach and the crashing waves or being away from home. Either way, I wanted to kiss Ben.

He turned and looked at me with crunched eyebrows as if waiting for the end of a joke.

"I'm serious," I continued. "We are good friends; we know exactly where the other stands when it comes to relationships. What could be the harm in a kiss?"

I stared at Ben waiting for a reply, his face turned expressionless. I like to think that I could always read him but at that moment he had a really good poker face.

"Okay," he quietly agreed. We said nothing else and turned to face each other. I took a step toward him and leaned forward a little on my toes to reach him. I pulled back my long, wavy hair and gave him a quick kiss on the lips.

As I pulled away he grabbed me, one arm around my waist, the other gently grabbed the back of my neck and he pulled me into him. I closed my eyes as I felt his soft lips, cold from the breeze, become warm. He kissed slowly and softly. I could feel the stubble from his face. Surprisingly, it felt good as it tickled just slightly.

I didn't know what to do with my hands, and somehow, they both ended up on his chest. I could feel his heart beating fast.

I pushed away slowly to catch my breath. As he stared into my eyes, I became so confused. This felt like more than a kiss.

I stepped back and removed my hands from his chest. He reluctantly removed his arm from around my waist. I felt a little shaky in the knees; lightheaded even. I felt something that I shouldn't have.

We continued to stare at each other for a while. I wanted to say something, but I was frozen. Should I laugh? But this wasn't funny. Did he feel it, too? He must have. Why did I agree to a kiss? I have to say something. Say something!

Ben took a step toward me. I interrupted his movements, "Well, I guess we should go back to the hotel room," I blurted out.

He looked at me with raised eyebrows. "Separate rooms. Hotel rooms, separately, together."

I stumbled through my words. "Let's head back and check on the kids," I continued with awkward hand movements.

Now here I am, a year later, bringing up the embarrassing past. My phone buzzed as I hid under the covers. Of course, it was Ben.

Good morning sunshine, feelin' better? That was quite a scene you made in the bathroom yesterday.

Did he mean the loud barfing and dry heaving? Or when I hit on him? I decided to not answer. I heard a soft knock on my door, followed by two sweet voices entering my room.

We shared a suite that had a large sitting room and kitchen area in the middle with two private bedrooms on either side.

"Mom, wake up," Mellie said happily.

"Wake up, Madelyn," Caroline said after her. They both jumped on my bed.

"Caroline, are you walking around the hotel in your pajamas?" I asked.

"No, I stayed in Mellie's room last night. My Dad wanted me to share with Heather, but I just couldn't do it. She's annoying," Caroline complained. I laughed at her honesty, and that made me feel better.

"Let's go, Mom. Get ready! We have a long day ahead of us," Mellie said with excitement.

Chapter Five

First on the itinerary of my very well-organized daughter was sightseeing. One of my favorite qualities about Mellie was that she was so on top of everything, without being too bossy; not a trait she received from me.

We gathered downstairs in the lobby at the Pierre A Taj Hotel. Perfect place to hold a wedding. Heather had recommended it. I was reluctant to listen to her suggestion, but she actually did well.

For a split second, I entertained the idea that Heather and I could be good friends. I was distracted by the complimentary chocolates at the front desk which made me love this place even more.

It was winter in New York City; a drastic change from what we were all used to in Arizona. But we came prepared to survive. The knowledge that I would get a New York Christmas made all the cold worth it.

Across the street from the hotel was the entrance to south

Central Park. Food trucks and vendors lined the sidewalks before the opening to the park and the aroma of sweet vanilla and fruit filled my lungs. The source was a small food truck of Belgium waffles and ice cream. This seemed like a perfect way to start off our tour.

I tried not to look straight at Ben. I know I can't ignore him this whole trip, but maybe if we just don't talk for a while, I won't feel so stupid.

"Hey, did you get my message this morning?" he said walking straight toward me and away from the others.

"Yes," I mumbled as I shoved a big spoonful of ice cream and chocolate drizzle in my mouth. Bus and truck tires screeched through the streets. Steam came up from the manholes. Loud horns honking made it so that Ben had to stand closer to me so that I could hear him. A gush of cold air blew over me along with the smell of sewer and exhaust. The leaves were gone from the trees in Central Park, but I could still see the beauty of nature. A huge contrast from the crowded streets and sidewalks.

"And?" Ben gestured with his hands for me to continue.

"Sorry; I didn't know what to say. I'm a little embarrassed." I put my concentration back on my waffle, and not him.

"Maddie, it's me. I've seen you puke before, I've seen you cry a million times. I've seen you without makeup. Hell! I've even seen you naked!" I choked on my ice cream, surprised at his bold response.

It's true though; he did see me completely naked. I invited him over for breakfast months ago, after we finished a three-mile run.

In my defense, I told him to come back in thirty minutes, so I could take a quick shower. We have an open-door policy between our families.

I had just finished my shower and realized that I didn't have any clean towels. I tiptoed quickly to the laundry room, but before I could grab a towel out of the basket, the door to the garage flew open, and there was Benny; frozen in time, eyes locked to my wet body.

We made eye contact momentarily before I let out a yelp and promptly turned to run back to my room. We didn't have breakfast together that morning. We didn't talk or text each other for about two weeks after that, never bringing it up again. Until now.

"Oh my gosh Benny, why did you bring that up? Is it 'let's talk about Maddie's embarrassing moments day'?" I snapped, still trying not to look directly at him. A few pigeons that had been snacking on crumbs nearby flew off at my loud reply.

I looked over and noticed Heather looking our way, but Jared seemed to keep her busy in deep conversation about something. Part of me wanted her to come and end this horrible discussion while the other part of me didn't want any chance of her hearing it.

"I'm just saying, I'm your best friend; I've seen you at your worst and your best." He smirked and then winked at me. "I didn't tell anyone about that day after our run or what happened on the plane." He continued, "Secrets between best friends."

"You didn't tell Heather?" I was surprised. I looked back over to where the kids and Heather had been standing. They had moved over to some street vendors and admired some of the paintings.

"What? About seeing you naked?" he replied.

"No, Benny! About the plane," I said, choking again on my ice cream waffle.

"Nope," he said hiding a smile.

Why was he suddenly feeling so bold to bring up such things? Maybe it was the cold air, or maybe Heather gave him the same pill she gave me? I just looked at him and smiled. He was loyal to me, and I felt so lucky to know him.

After we ate our waffles and had some light conversation about the cold, Mellie told us her plans for the rest of the day.

We started across the street at the Plaza Hotel. It was more beautiful than I imagined. I had seen the hotel in movies but the details inside were exquisite; the large glass chandeliers, enormous pillars that lined the entry way, and glass windows that filled the sky above the eating area. There were little shops inside; one sold perfumes; scents some of the old Hollywood stars used to wear.

I thought it was so exciting, I was in heaven.

"Oh yes, they're very expensive; I have a few of them at home," Heather said quickly. I felt Benny's gaze on me. He smiled, admiring my excitement over the bewitching perfume bottles.

"Maybe I'll buy one before we leave," I said. "These are classy."

Our next stop was FAO Schwartz Toy store. Mellie and I could have stayed there all day. We played with all the display toys we could get our hands on. We laughed and joked about things from the past. Made fun of each other.

All of us seemed to be having a good time except for Heather, who just stood there. She looked bored. I realized that she probably felt left out from our inside jokes and friendly insults. She hadn't tried to be a part of it, which made her even harder for me to read. I'd reluctantly tried to get to know her in the past. I'd only ever heard bad things from the girls and good things from Ben. I guess I needed to find out for myself.

"What do you think of this place?" I said as I approached Heather.

She smiled. "Oh, it's great. I guess I'm just not that into toys and candy." She waved her hand around pointing at nothing in particular.

I opened my mouth in an attempt to exchange good dialogue, when I was abruptly interrupted by a candy cinnamon bear flying in front of my face and hitting Jared in the back of the head.

I backed away, realizing it was Mellie who had thrown it. She and Caroline ducked behind a pole waiting to see Jared's response. Benny took sides with Jared and a big gum ball came flying toward my face. I took cover with the girls. Heather backed away from the situation with a look of shock. The girls handed me some cinnamon bears and I snuck around the other side of a pole while the girls threw their last few at the boys. I got close behind Benny and took my shot, square in the back of the head. I tried to run, but he grabbed my wrists and I could not stop laughing.

Heather marched up behind us. "What on earth are you doing?" she hissed angrily; her cheeks flamed with her embarrassment. "Do you want to get kicked out of here?" she whispered and grabbed Ben by the arm.

We stopped immediately, like school children being disciplined by the principal. Heads down, hands behind our backs.

Caroline quickly walked past me with a smirk and rolled her eyes. Jared and Mellie quickly followed with their heads down and silent giggles. Heather led Ben out the side door. I stayed behind to make my purchases, getting another scolding from the checkout clerk. I could see Heather talking to Ben with small hand gestures. She didn't look too mad, mostly just embarrassed to be with us.

The three kids were bundled together, trying each other's candy, when I walked outside. Ben and Heather were standing next to each other, not talking. He flashed me an 'I got in trouble look'. I couldn't help but laugh a little.

"Where to next?" Heather asked kindly, arms crossed and eager to move on.

"Tiffany's; right across the street." Caroline stammered.

"Oh good, my favorite place." Heather perked up and led our group down to the crosswalk. She strolled in like she owned the store. Her hands quickly flew to her face like she'd just walked into her own surprise party. "Oh, Benny, look how divine." This was her toy store.

Benny? I had no idea how much that would sting to hear that coming from her lips. He's *my* Benny. I watched her gleam and laugh over all the diamonds. She held tight to Benny's arm as they slowly walked around the room.

There were many display cases filled with jewelry. Heather found herself in front of the biggest diamond ring she could find; it was gold with a single round diamond, and very expensive. "If I were to choose a ring for myself, it would be this one," Heather said, turning to Benny with a hinting smile. I could see Caroline in the background imitating her actions and Mellie and Jared laughed.

I felt a little bad for Heather. She didn't seem like a bad person, just different. She actually seemed nice. And what if she became one of the family someday? I gave the kids the "you'd-better-be-nice look."

I decided to chime in. "That is a very beautiful ring, Heather. I hope you get one like that someday."

Everyone seemed surprised at my response, especially Heather. "Thanks, Madelyn." She smiled at me with appreciation.

Mellie popped up from behind. "What ring would you pick Mom?"

I felt Benny's gaze of interest. This was a conversation that we never had, either. "Uhm," I walked around the case slowly with a hand to my chin and found a single gold band.

"This one; simple and beautiful. I could run with this one."

Ben smiled and nodded his head in agreement. I could feel Heather's gaze on him and then on me. It felt uncomfortable.

Later, we had lunch in Central Park; hot dogs from a small food truck, with everything on it. It wasn't great, but at least I could say I'd tried it. We sat on a short wall overlooking what should be a lawn of grass but was now covered by a thin sheet of snow. I bundled myself in my coat and rewrapped my scarf around my neck.

"What are you thinking about?" Jared asked me. I looked over to Mellie and Caroline chatting about something and then over to Heather and Ben holding hands and cuddling on a bench near a bridge.

"I'm just thinking about how perfect this place is, and how life changes so quickly." I smiled, looking back at him.

"Are you happy?" he questioned, very seriously.

I was quite taken aback by his boldness. "Yes; yes, I am," I said, sitting up more. He gave me a weak smile.

"I would like to ask you the same question, but I think it would be pointless," I continued.

He laughed. "Yes, I'm very happy. It took me a long time to get there after Mom died, but you and Mellie are a big part of bringing happiness back into my life. And the life of my family," he said.

I smiled and patted his shoulder. His trials had made him thoughtful and kind.

Jared stood, facing in the direction of his Dad and Heather. "I don't think my Dad is as happy as he could be."

I stood next to Jared, "Well, I understand that; there's always a missing piece after a loved one dies."

"I think he could be completely happy again, if someone I know and love lets her stubbornness go." He looked back at me with his big brown eyes.

I said nothing but just smiled back and then looked over at Heather, who now had her head on Ben's shoulder and was intertwining her hand in his.

After lunch we took a long walk through the park. Steam came up from the small lakes. Joggers and bike riders passed by us. It felt peaceful inside the park; a huge contrast from the bustling city streets. Heather tried harder to connect with the kids. I helped when I could, but it was not an easy task.

We ended up at the Natural History Museum that was located on the west side of Central Park. It was my favorite stop. I broke off from the rest of the group when we got inside, so

I could have some time to myself. We spent almost three hours there, exploring the rooms and exhibits. Well, *I* spent three hours there. I realized it was 4 pm and quickly ran back to the front steps, finding everyone waiting there for me. "I'm so sorry, I lost track of time, and then I just, well, I just got lost. I'm so sorry."

"We aren't mad Mom. We know how excited you get about *everything!*" Mellie said, laughing, and everyone followed suit. Well, everyone except for Heather.

"We tried to call you over and over." Heather tried to say it like she'd been concerned, but to me it sounded more like a parent reprimanding a teenager.

"I am really sorry," I said again, trying not to laugh at Caroline in the background, imitating Heather. "The sign at the front said to put phones on silent, and then I just completely forgot."

I really needed to stop laughing at Caroline making fun of Heather. She wasn't so bad, but I just couldn't help myself. I vowed right then that I would try harder to be Heather's advocate.

Afterwards, we walked back to our hotel through Central Park. Heather didn't let go of Benny; clutching his arm and giggling into his ear. He smiled and laughed, too. Even though I was unsure of my feelings for her, I tried to tell myself that she might be good for him. She wasn't what I pictured he would choose, but I guess the only person I could see with him was his sweet wife, who had already passed on.

What does he see in Heather? I wondered. She hates running, hiking, and basically anything outdoors. She is super serious and awkward around the kids. Maybe that's because she's never been married and has no children of her own.

She's been in school for many years while working her way up to an executive job in some marketing company I've never heard of. Why does this bother me so much?

That evening as I lay awake thinking about the events of the day, I heard a knock at my door. I quickly put on my robe as I scurried to see who was there. "Heather, what a surprise," I said.

"Yes, well, I was thinking that maybe me and you could spend the day tomorrow, together, just the two of us," Heather muttered, not quite looking at me.

I paused for a few seconds trying to make sense of her words, "Oh, uhm, okay, but I'm not sure what the kids had planned."

"I already arranged it with them," Heather said quickly.

I couldn't see any way out of this. "Oh, well then, great; me and you." I struggled to get my words out and smile.

"I just figured that since we'll probably be seeing a lot more of each other in the near future, being a part of the same family possibly, that we should get more acquainted," she said looking down at the floor and then up to the ceiling.

Was she scared of me? Why wouldn't she look at me? And what's with 'more acquainted'? First of all, who says that? Second, no, I do not want to get 'more acquainted' with you. Say no! *Say NO!*

"Yes, that would be lovely," I said with a forced smile. Lovely? Who says lovely? What am I doing? *What am I turning into?*

"Great," Heather said, finally looking at me, "I'll call you in the morning."

I plopped back in my bed dreading what tomorrow would bring. I knew I should try and get to know her. I wanted to set a good example to the kids, but the idea of spending a day with her alone sounded miserable. I can do this, I thought to myself.

My phone buzzed. It was Benny.

Today was fun.

I laughed out loud as I texted back.

I loved every minute of it, especially the moment I hit you with a cinnamon bear.

You know I'll get you back, right?

Oh, I'm counting on it.

Chapter Six

I tried to have a positive attitude the next morning as I took the elevator down to my presumed death. We had breakfast at the same waffle truck by my request. Followed by a day of shopping on Fifth Avenue. What could be better?

We had a lot of small talk, mostly about her and her accomplishments. I hated to admit that she seemed nicer than I thought, but my heart would not let me like her. She asked me a lot of questions about myself and seemed genuinely interested in my friendship with Ben.

My phone buzzed. It was a selfie of the kids on something called *The Beast*, a speed boat that takes you around the Statue of Liberty. I burst out laughing at their silly faces. I showed Heather and she smiled.

As we continued shopping, I learned she was an only child who'd been expected to know how to do everything. She was an accomplished pianist, violinist, swimmer, and gymnast. Her Spanish and French are as good as her English. She earned a Bachelors, Masters, and PhD in something I can't even pronounce. We browsed through many stores talking about her talents and education. I understood more now of her seriousness. She asked about my accomplishments.

I laughed. "I know how to down-shift my car so I can do 180 spins in the parking lot." What was I going to say, I'm a mom and I help teenagers get their act together? I felt I didn't have any accomplishments to compare with hers, and I wanted to lighten the mood. She was not amused.

She set up tea for us at a restaurant called *Tavern on the Green.* We took a taxi there and she talked about different sights along the way. She told me she knows the head chef who reserved the best view for us. It was in fact a gorgeous view of Central Park.

Tea was brought to us soon after we sat down at the table.

"Could I get a large Coke please?" I asked as the waiter poured the steaming drink into my cup.

Heather didn't say anything but shot me a look of disapproval. I felt uncomfortable being around such a classy lady.

After some more small talk and a little bit of silence, "I love Benny, you know," Heather blurted out as she sat her cup down.

I choked a little on my drink. *Oh, please don't go there,* I was begging her in my mind; *please don't go there.*

"And he loves me," Heather continued. "He's going to propose to me soon; I can feel it."

She went there; I can't believe she went there. "I am happy for you both," I lied.

Her whole demeanor changed. No more Ms. Fake Nice Lady.

"Are you?" Heather said sarcastically as she tilted her

head to the side. Her perfectly curled blonde hair bounced back and forth.

"Of course, I am; why wouldn't I be?" I continued with the lie and stared into my Coke glass.

"Because I think you're in love with Ben and are stringing him along because you don't want to get married. Ben told me about your weird pact or commitment-thing you made with yourself."

I could feel my eyes widen as I took a deep breath.

"We would have already been married or engaged by now if you weren't in the picture." Heather straightened her head putting both arms on the table and giving me a stern look.

"WOW! I don't even know what to say right now. This is absolutely silly; me and Benny are friends—"

"Best friends!" she insisted.

"Best friends," I agreed, "but that doesn't mean I'm in love with him."

"I love him, Madelyn. I know I can make him happy and it would be easier if you weren't distracting him every time I turned around." Heather was almost yelling.

I was in shock and so offended. How do I respond? Say something! Do something! All I could think about was jumping across the table and choking her. "I—" I couldn't get any words out. And to think I had started to like the woman.

"Also, I don't think you should call him Benny anymore, it doesn't seem right for anyone else to call him that but me," she said, still with both arms on the table leaning closely into me.

I got up so fast I shook the table spilling some of the drinks.

"Okay," I said quickly. "This was fun, Heather; thank you

for a very unforgettable day." I grabbed my bag and walked backward away from the table, then turned quickly to get out of the restaurant as fast as I could. I could hear Heather telling me to wait and maybe she even followed me, I'm not sure. All I knew was that I needed some space to breathe. I kept walking until I realized that I was not only lost somewhere in Central Park but that I left my coat in the restaurant.

What just happened? I was so mad! I paced in front of some large trees contemplating all the things that I should have said to her. "First of all, he is *my* Benny. I can make him happy; he loves me," I whispered to myself while pacing and hand gesturing. I noticed two homeless men staring at me, so I decided to sit down on a bench and stop talking to myself. I quickly stood up again realizing how cold I was and continued my pacing.

"What am I saying? I don't mean that. He isn't mine; he doesn't love me, and I don't love him. *Ugh!* That woman makes me so mad." I eventually sat back down on the bench with the two homeless men still staring and awaiting my next act. I stood up again and patrolled back and forth trying to breathe. The tears that rolled down my face felt cold; when I went to wipe them away I realized it was snowing.

My phone buzzed. It was Ben.

How goes the girls' day? Hope you are having fun? Did I mention that everyone left me by myself?

I didn't know what to say to him, there had been things that had never been brought up between us. I decided to just be honest.

It went ok to bad.

What happened?

I could almost feel his concern.

I absolutely do not know how to talk to you about it.

I wished I had just ignored his text.

Try.

What if you talk to Heather about it first? Then we can talk about it if you want to later.

Maddie!

I wish I never said anything.

Maddie!

She loves you ok, she loves you and wants to marry you and make you happy and she wants me to stop calling you Benny and stop distracting you and stop being your best friend.

I sent it before I could change my mind.

Quite a few minutes passed without a response from Benny. A cold breeze passed over me reminding me that I forgot my coat. I just kept staring at my phone biting my lip. I finally texted him again.

Benny, you there?

I'm here, I just don't know what to say.

I don't want things to change Benny. We are good together just the way we are, our families are a great team. I want us to grow old down the street from each other and raise grandchildren and be happy. I'm crying by the way.

The two homeless men that had watched my acting debut earlier walked off, shaking their heads at my quivering body and tearful eyes.

Where are you? I am coming to get you.

I don't know, I'm lost in Central Park and I am freezing.

Since our hotel is across the street from the Park it didn't take long for him to find me with the few descriptions I gave him. As soon as he came into view the tears started pouring down my face once again. Benny was no stranger to seeing my cry. Every year on the anniversary of my husband's death I was a mess of tears.

> *This past anniversary he came over to be with me, showing up at my door unannounced. He even knocked, which he usually doesn't do. He and I said nothing to each other when I opened the door. He made me dinner and then we watched a movie on the couch. I fell asleep and he carried me to my room. I had put some blankets and a pillow on the couch for him but at some time during the night he heard me crying. I know because he came in and laid next to me and just held me. He told me to just cry and that everything would be all right. He caressed my face and wiped my tears. He was gone before I woke the next morning and we never said anything about it again.*

Chapter Seven

As soon as he reached me, he wrapped his coat around me and embraced me. I cried into his shoulder and neck. After a few minutes my sobs slowed and he pulled me back looking at my pathetic face.

"Let's go somewhere," he said.

"Where?" I said as I wiped my cheeks dry.

"Anywhere; we're in New York City; we could go anywhere and do anything you want." He smiled, standing and stretching his arms out wide.

I smiled. "Well, I have always wanted to visit the New York Library."

"The library, seriously?" He put his arms down. "We are in New York City and you want to go to the library?"

"Yes!" I yelled with a laugh. I was already feeling better; Benny always had that effect on me.

We walked all the way there. It wasn't too far, maybe about a mile from our hotel, stopping at a chocolate store on the way. Chocolate always made me feel better. Chocolate and Coke. I knew at some point we would have to talk about what happened, but I wanted to just enjoy these next moments.

The library was exquisite. I kept spinning and staring at the beautiful architecture. I kept touching all the books and just talking about everything I saw. Benny just watched me with a smile on his face. We proceeded to explore the library. The aisles of books were mesmerizing to me. After a few minutes of reading titles Benny whispered to me "Maddie, we need to talk." With a book in my hand I turned and looked at Benny.

"I know, I just wanted to delay it as long as I could."

"Why?" He asked.

I sighed. "Because everything is changing Benny; our life, our friendship as we know it will never be the same. I won't be able to text you in the middle of the night to kill a spider."

He laughed.

"Or go running with you, or do family trips to California. Everything, Benny, we do everything together."

"Maddie, it doesn't have to change, you know that."

"Only if you don't marry her." I fiddled with the book I was holding.

He folded his arms. "Maddie, I want to be married, I like being married."

"You want to get married again?" I stopped toying with the book and sat it down on a shelf.

"Yes." He replied as if he had spent hours trying to explain something to me only for me to just barely get it.

"Since when?" I crossed my arms this time. "I thought we wanted the same thing?"

"I did, at first." His arms going from being folded to one touching the back of his neck and the other rubbing the stubble on his chin. "But then I realized how wonderful it would be to get married again, to a woman I love."

"Someone like Heather," I said quietly, looking back at the book I laid on the shelf.

"Maybe."

"Do you love her?" I looked directly at him.

"It's not that easy, Maddie." Still playing with his chin.

"Either you love someone, or you don't." I shrugged my shoulders.

"Do you love me?" he asked.

At some point during our intense conversation, I found myself backed against a shelf. Benny was now standing directly in front of me.

"Yes, you know I do," I said, quickly looking down at the ground, not knowing what to do with my hands.

"How? How do you love me?" He stepped closer.

"Benny." I finally crossed my arms in front of me to keep from shaking.

"How; how do you love me?" he repeated, slower and unrelenting.

My heart ached, confused, frustrated. I sensed the palms of my hands starting to sweat. I didn't know how I felt anymore. Until Heather, I didn't let myself even explore those feelings. Well, at least not often.

"Maddie, it was you that made me want to fall in love again. You, who made me realize it was possible. You are beautiful, loving, fun, and kind. You are silly, and ridiculous, and make me laugh. I love that you get lost and lose track of time. I love to watch you get excited about things like perfume bottles and library books, and the way you love chocolate and running and our children."

A warm tingling filled my heart to hear him say 'our children'.

He continued "I couldn't tell you the moment I fell in love with you, but it happened; it just happened."

"You're in love with me?" I questioned.

"Yes." He seemed almost frustrated waving his arms up in the air. "How could you not know, the way I talk to you, look at you, our kiss; oh, man, that kiss, how did you not feel anything when we kissed?"

He was pacing now but I was too scared to move. I felt ridiculous that I hadn't realized his feelings before.

"I never said I didn't feel anything, it's just not what I wanted, you knew that, you've always known that."

Now he was back standing in front of me with his hands on my shoulders. "I have always known that Maddie, which is why I never crossed that line, why I dated other women, why I am dating Heather; but I am so madly in love with you it hurts, I want to hold you, kiss you. I want to marry you, Maddie. I want our family to go on vacations together and get in candy fights together, I want you; I love you."

I was in shock; my heart was so confused. I didn't let myself feel this way for Benny but knew there was something there. I made a commitment to never love again. That's what I want, isn't it? How else can I be loyal to Luke? How else can I keep my marriage vows? I felt brave enough to move away from his hold, pacing myself this time.

"If you are in love with me," I stopped, turning to look at him, "then what is Heather to you? I don't understand."

"Heather is what came along because I can't have you. I

do love her, in a different way, and I can see a future with her. I think she could make me happy, I could make her happy. I didn't fall in love with her the way I fell in love with you. It took me a long time and it's different. With her I see the possibility of a future."

I turned my body from him. I couldn't face him to tell him what I felt I needed to. I couldn't bear to see him in pain as I had so many times before. But to be the actual cause of it would be more than I could handle. "Benny, I can't," I whispered with my head facing down to the floor, tears flowing from my eyes. "I'm sorry, I'm so very sorry."

Everything was still and silent. I felt him tilt a little and then sigh, and then, after a few long, agonizing moments, I heard him walk away. I didn't move for a long time. I looked up to make sure he had gone, and then sat down on the floor, leaned my head up against the book shelf and cried. What have I done? What have I done? Hours passed.

I took a taxi back to the hotel hoping I wouldn't see anybody. My heart hurt in confusion. I knew I had feelings for Benny but was torn between them and the commitment I made to myself after Luke died. So many questions ran through my mind. Why didn't Benny tell me before? Was he afraid I would stop being his friend? Was I leading him on? So many memories kept coming back, making me realize how much Benny loved me, and how he did look at me, does look at me. How could I be so stupid and blind? I was stringing him along. We were living a life together as if we were married minus all the mushy stuff. I know I had thought about kissing Benny before and holding him. But I always locked those feelings out. *I don't know what I want. I am so confused.*

The kids were not back to the hotel yet. I changed into an

old comfy shirt and hid myself under the covers of my warm bed. A knock at the door jolted me up. Who could that be? I panicked a little. I threw on my robe and opened the door. It was someone from the hotel with a box from FAO Schwartz.

"This was delivered to the front desk early this morning and we waited until you returned to bring it up." He smiled and handed me the package. He was maybe in his 20's and had a slight gap in his front teeth. He also had a strong New York accent. I imagined him wearing a backwards cap and baggy jeans on his days off. I opened the box to find a container filled with cinnamon bears and a note that said *It's not over, watch your back.* It was signed *B*.

"Oh Benny," I whispered through a sob. I've been such an idiot and what a mess I have made. Not even chocolate or soda could help me through this. That night I could hardly sleep. I tossed and turned in bed trying to sort my feelings. I knew I loved him, but I wasn't sure exactly how I loved him.

At some point during my pity party I fell asleep. I dreamt I was a dinosaur who was happily eating leaves with my family when along came a T-rex and ate every family member and then laughed at me. I jolted out of bed in a sweat around three am. I was grateful it was only a dream.

I took deep breaths and sat there in silence for a while. I felt as if my feelings were uncovering themselves. Like a bandage was being removed from my heart and it was ready to function again. Could it be this simple and easy? "Could I love Benny?" I whispered to myself, "Do I love him?"

I pictured a life without him and it made my stomach hurt thinking about him sharing a future with Heather. "I love him," I whispered to myself. "I do love him; I love Benny," I said loudly, laughing at the realization. I felt a sense of freedom saying that out loud.

I've loved him for a long time. I knew it but wouldn't let my heart know it. It was obvious, I had just been so stubborn and closed off. We were already a family. We belonged together. I love him the way he loves me. I let out another small laugh and smiled. It felt good to feel that and to not feel guilty about it. "I love him, I love him!" The more I said it out loud, the more certain I was, the more it felt safe. It didn't feel wrong. I needed to tell him, to talk to him right away.

I grabbed my phone and texted him.

Come into the hall, I need to talk to you.

Minutes passed. Nothing. I waited for what seemed like forever. He was probably sleeping. I needed to wake him up; this couldn't wait. I walked across the hall to his room and knocked on the door. Again nothing, he must be in a deep sleep.

I looked down and realized how inappropriately dressed I was. I had on a gray t-shirt and blue lace underwear. "Crap!" I said under my breath. I turned back to my room only to find the door locked. I looked for my phone; then realized I'd left it on my bed. "Crap, crap, crap!" I knocked on my room door, hoping that one of the girls might hear from the adjoining suite. *This isn't happening.*

The elevator door suddenly opened, and I felt my throat sink to the bottom of my stomach. I heard a loud donkey laugh coming from down the hall.

"This isn't happening," I whispered looking around for somewhere to hide. "This can *not* be happening. No, no, no," I whispered again to myself, trying to lift a plant off the end table to hide myself. I heard Benny laugh next. There was nowhere to hide so I just stood there, my back to the door and waited for one of the worst days of my lives to continue on to the next. I closed my eyes hoping that somehow, they would either pass me by or I would wake up back in my bed from another bad dream.

"Madelyn! What are you doing?" Heather sounded very surprised.

I opened my eyes. Both expressed looks of shock across their faces.

"I, uhm, was checking to see if they brought me a newspaper, and I locked myself out; ha, ha." I shook from embarrassment.

Benny just gave me an unbelieving look. He knew I was lying. I realized he hadn't checked his phone and I didn't know what else to say.

"I'll call downstairs and get you a key." Ben said, walking back toward his room.

"Thanks Benny…Ben. Thanks, Ben." I gave Heather a half smile still moving awkwardly.

Heather shook her head and gave me an approving smile. Ben disappeared into his room.

Heather walked slowly past me, popping her knuckles with her head down. "These are the distractions I am talking about that will stop as soon as we are married." Heather looked back up at me, putting her hands behind her back and standing at ease.

Ben came out of his hotel room and handed me a robe. He didn't look at me. "They'll be right up." He turned back around to go to his room but not before Heather grabbed him and gave him a long goodnight kiss. "I will see you in the morning," she gloated.

He smiled back at her and then quietly disappeared again into his room. She turned and looked my way and smiled as if she had just conquered the world. And maybe she had. The elevator door opened again shortly after. It was the same boy who delivered the box earlier the night before. He didn't look at me funny or say a word. He opened the door for me and I thanked him graciously. I turned to go into my room and then stopped. I twirled back around to Heather. She was still waiting in front of her door, flashing me a deceitful smile.

I stared at her for a minute. "I hate you," I said loud and clear. Her face lit up in surprise and anger. I quickly went through my door and shut it behind me before she could respond, or at least before I could hear her respond.

Why can't I just be normal? I thought to myself. My phone buzzed, it was Benny.

It's too late; I'm sorry.

I didn't reply. I didn't want to argue. I felt like we had done a lot of that already.

The remaining hours were miserable. I hardly slept, feeling that I completely ruined everything. *It's too late, I'm sorry,* kept haunting my mind. Did he mean it was too late into the night or that it was too late for us?

I felt like a heavy brick lay in the bottom of my stomach. I kept wondering if being in New York City was confusing my emotions. Maybe when I go home, things will go back to normal and I will be able to hold those feelings in once again. Who am I kidding? I have now opened a previously jammed door that's going to be impossible to close again.

Chapter Eight

Mellie jumped on my bed the next morning; she was so excited for the day. A lot of the guests would be arriving today for the special rehearsal dinner taking place tonight. If it was any other day, I would have pretended to be sick and lay in bed. But I couldn't today, or tomorrow. I didn't want to tell Mellie. I didn't want to tell anyone.

I sent the girls off to breakfast in the dining hall early so that I could come down a short while later. I needed to try and get the puffiness out of my eyes and collect myself. Mostly I just wanted to run; to run and not stop.

When I entered the room, everyone was gathered at a round table. Much different atmosphere from the waffle truck across the street. The room was filled with flowers and elegant curtains filled the windows. White linens covered the tables beneath china dishes. Everyone seemed to be in deep discussion about something. Laughter and surprise, a happy discussion.

Silence fell over the table as I approached. Jared looked at me and gave me a pity smile. He quickly got up and pulled a chair out for me. "Hey, Mom," he said, patting my back. Be still my heart. That felt good to hear.

"What is it," I asked; "what did I miss?" I hoped no one noticed my puffy eyes. Still silence resumed. I looked around and no one would meet my gaze, except Heather. She smiled at me while I sat down across from her. Not the friendly smile, the I'm-going-to-get-you smile.

"You haven't heard I guess; I figured Benny would have texted you about it." She patted Benny on the shoulder. I adjusted myself in my chair patiently waiting. I grabbed a glass of water and took a sip. "We're engaged!" she yelled and then laughed her donkey laugh.

I spit water from my mouth and nose. *I keep doing that.* I was choking and my nose was burning. I tried to get myself under control. I coughingly congratulated them. No one else spoke, they just watched me cautiously. When I got my hacking under control, I congratulated them again.

"I am so happy for you," I forced myself to say with a smile. I looked at Ben and he flashed me an I-feel-sorry-for-you smile. "When did you propose?" I asked Benny with careful composure.

"Last night!" Heather yelled excitedly before Benny could even attempt to get a word in. *Last night,* I thought to myself. That must have been where they were so late. I didn't even notice a ring. I was too wrapped up in my own embarrassment to notice. I wonder why she didn't rub it in my face then?

"At the top of the Empire State Building," she continued

loudly for the whole room to hear. I nodded my head in agreement.

"It was perfect." She started using her hands to go along with her story-telling animation. She looked at Benny. "He told me he loved me and that we'll be happy together." She stuck her ring out for everyone to see and gushed.

It was a gold ring with a round diamond; not as big as the one she wanted in Tiffany's, but it was just as classy. Heather turned and kissed Benny on the cheek. It all made sense to me now. *It's too late, I'm sorry.* He had already proposed.

"Well, that's wonderful," I said as I put my napkin on my lap. I was sick to my stomach, but I didn't want to cause a scene. "Please pass the croissants, Caroline," I said.

No one else hardly said a word except for Heather rambling about their future together. The children would nod and smile, and Mellie would nudge my knee under the table every once in a while. I would just grab her hand and squeeze it. I could see Benny look my way a few times. I'm sure even in his frustration toward me, he still cared about how I was doing and feeling.

In the middle of Heather's ramblings, Mellie screamed, "Uncle Todd!" She scrambled out of her seat and dashed toward him. I looked up from the table to see Luke's younger brother standing in the doorway arms wide open ready to intercept his favorite niece. I glanced at Ben who was already looking at me in concern. The concern turned to anger as he looked back at Todd.

Just over a year ago, before our trip to California, Todd came for a visit. He ended up staying two months at my house. He had some excuse about his home being renovated and that it was taking longer than he thought.

It was a poor excuse, but I didn't really mind at first. I knew Ben didn't like it. Todd flirted with me non-stop. He was a two-time divorcee. He's been a big flirt as long as I could remember.

It was endearing when we were younger, and I was dating Luke; it almost felt innocent. But as the years went by, and especially after his visit, I just felt like he was a big pervert.

He's very handsome, and the ladies love him. He looked a lot like Luke, which made it hard for me to fight off his advances. On a night that I had forgotten I invited Ben over, Todd was already sitting next to me on the couch flirting in his usual way.

I'm not quite sure how it happened, but Ben walked in right as Todd had been trying to show me some magic trick placing his head close to mine. He grabbed my head, pulled me in, and kissed me. Ben cleared his throat loudly and I jumped up from the couch. I didn't want that kiss, nor did I like it. It felt nothing like Luke's.

In embarrassment I walked to my room and shut the door. I didn't come out until the next morning. When I finally did, Todd had already packed and left. I asked him about it later at which time he referred me to Ben to discuss the matter. I was too scared to ask, so it became one more thing on our awkward list that we didn't talk about.

Mellie brought Todd back toward our table. I stood up as he came closer and I tried to give him a quick side hug. I was very surprised he'd showed up. We'd sent him an invitation of course, but he never told us he was coming. I even tried to be strategic and send it late so that it would be inconvenient for him to plan a trip.

He picked me up in a hug then smacked my butt as he sat me back down. "It's good to see you, Sugar Lips." He winked at me. My face burned hot.

Ben's face turned red with anger as he glared at Todd. Heather watched with interest and amusement.

"Ben," Todd said, smiling and offering a hand shake.

"Todd," Ben said, not smiling and not offering his hand back.

"And who is this beautiful woman to your right?" He turned his attention to Heather.

"This is…" Ben couldn't quite get the word out.

"Heather; my name is Heather and I'm Ben's fiancée." She stood and shook his hand smiling and giggling.

Todd looked at Ben in surprise and then over at me in confusion. This trip just keeps getting worse.

"Well, isn't she the most beautiful thing I've ever seen, well, after Mellie of course." He looked back at Mellie with a wink. He sat with us for over an hour, talking about his latest travels and women. Heather had so many questions for him and seemed to be intrigued by his charm.

Like Ben, Jared was not amused. He kept looking over at me and rolling his eyes. It didn't faze Mellie and Caroline, they kept listening and laughing. Ben never spoke, he just sat there with a stoic look on his face. But I knew exactly what he was feeling.

I went to my room right after breakfast, making some lame excuse that I felt queasy. It was mostly true, though. I was quickly back in the same t-shirt, hiding under my covers again. It felt lonely to not to be getting texts from Ben. Maybe I will wake up at any moment realizing this was all a dream and that everything was how it used to be. I sat up in bed. I became aware that those were the same thoughts and patterns I had when Luke died.

But Ben isn't gone. I can do something to improve my happiness. It is not out of my control. I jumped out of bed, trying to think of a plan. *Now what?* I have to win him back somehow. It can't be too late.

Chapter Nine

I paced my room thinking up scenarios and possible outcomes. My door flew open. "Kitten, it's so good to see you." It was Todd. He looked over my outfit and then bounced his eyebrows at me.

"Todd, how did you get in here?" I moved to the other side of the bed to be further away from him.

"Waiting for Uncle Todd, I see," he said, flashing his eyes.

I slipped my robe on. "Do not ever refer to yourself as Uncle Todd like that; *ever*, its creepy; and I'm not your kitten! Seriously, how did you get in here? And get out!" I said angrily, and still surprised.

"I got a key from Mellie," he laughed, flashing the card. "I told her I couldn't check into my room this early and I was tired," he said, smirking.

"Ok, you are a sneaky genius; now please leave," I begged.

"Sorry, I just missed you and wanted to talk to you. What are you doing?" He plopped himself on my bed, opening the magazine he had folded in his hand.

"I'm busy right now, Todd, can you please leave?" I asked, frustrated.

"Geez, I haven't heard from you in a year and this is the warm welcome I get." He flipped the pages of the magazine quickly as he laid back on my pillows. I stared at him sternly for a long while and then finally dared to ask, "What did Ben tell you the night you left my home?"

He put down his magazine and sat up a little. "What?" he sat back on my pillows putting the magazine down beside him. "You aren't still mad about that, are you, Sugar Lips?"

"I don't even know what to be mad about; what happened?" I suddenly realized I was yelling.

"Ben never told you?" He sat straight up.

"No," I softened and slowed my voice.

"Oh, it was nothing. He was mad I kissed you cuz he was in love with you. Something stupid like that. Which is one of the reasons I was so surprised to see Ben engaged to that very lovely Heather."

I glared at him once again. "I don't believe you."

He leaned back down in a comfortable position and picked up the magazine again.

"Get out, Todd, get out!" I was yelling again.

"What? It's fine." He started to slowly get off my bed.

"Get out! Get out! Get out!" I stomped my feet this time following him out the door to the hotel hallway. Ben and Heather were in the hall, talking. Heather looked at the both of us in amusement.

"Oh my, Madelyn what have you done now?" She was

laughing. Donkey laughing. Ben's stoic expression from earlier was replaced with surprise and what looked like irritation.

I slammed the door behind Todd and headed back to the comfort of my bed. But only for a little while because I came up with a plan.

Chapter Ten

I helped Mellie with last-minute arrangements before her dinner. With Caroline in tow we managed to fit in some pedicures. Caroline seemed a little more reserved than usual, but no one said anything about the engagement. I think they were trying to protect me.

"So, your Dad, huh? That's exciting." I said trying to break the awkwardness in the room.

"Yep," Caroline said with her head still in her magazine. Mellie flashed me a concerned look.

"I don't like her either, Caroline," I said quietly.

Caroline looked up from her magazine and smiled. Her smile quickly turned into a cry and then a sob. "I don't like her, Madelyn. I hate her so much; she is so mean and irritating." She continued to cry.

I put a hand on her leg. I would have embraced her had we not been in giant chairs with our feet soaking.

"Mom, this is surprising coming from you, I thought you

were okay with their relationship." Mellie sat up in her chair, sitting her phone down.

"I was; well, I thought I was, but I don't really think I ever was." I said hesitantly.

They both looked at me in confusion. I wanted to tell them but wasn't quite sure how to go about it.

"I like him." I finally got out. The girls both stared in anticipation, eyes wide open. "I love him!" I said loudly. "I love Ben; I love your dad." I laughed out loud and then almost cried.

The girls cheered. "It's about damn time, Mom," Mellie yelped and then sighed in relief.

"Do you know how long I've waited for you to say that?" Caroline asked, wiping tears from her eyes.

"Okay, I get it; I am a slow bloomer. But now what? He's engaged to Heather," I said.

"Do you want him?" Caroline asked. "Do you want to fight for him?"

"Yes; yes, I do," I said happily. I spent the next hour telling them about the events that took place the previous day and evening. We laughed and cried and schemed.

Later that afternoon, back in the hotel room, I helped Mellie get into her gorgeous evening gown that she bought for the rehearsal dinner. She grabbed my hand.

"Okay, Mom; you remember what we talked about? Your job is to look gorgeous and Caroline, Jared, and I will take care of the rest."

"I'm getting nervous: do you think I should just try and talk to him again?"

"Nope, a little jealousy never hurt anyone." She smiled, and I continued to pin up her beautiful hair.

"I guess I will be needing that second gown, then," I said, opening the closet.

Mellie laughed. "I told you so; I wish you'd have just listened to me the first time," she said.

We both laughed.

The gown was long, gray, and flowy, and hugged me in all the right places. I had to admit I looked gorgeous. I came into the dining hall thinking I'd make a grand entrance with my attractive gown and the statement it made, but still wasn't quite sure what exactly that statement was.

It didn't matter, because I was distracted by the beauty of the Reception Hall. Big glass-and-gold chandeliers hung from the ceilings, white and lavender flowers filled tables laid with gray and white linens. It was breathtaking.

As I slowly skimmed the room, I caught the eye of Benny. I guess I did make an entrance after all. He gave me a soft smile. I spun around in my dress and gave him a shoulder shrug. Before I could see his reaction, Caroline was at my side admiring my dress.

I made the rounds, talking to all our friends and family before we sat for dinner. I was seated next to Todd and across from Ben and Heather.

The salad was delicious. I was unsure of the kids' intentions for the night because they insisted on not telling me. But the table started off with some small talk about the city and the décor. Jared looked over at me and winked as if to notify me that something was about to happen.

"So, Heather, that's an interesting color in your hair." Her head shot up in embarrassment and anger.

"Yes, well, I don't know what happened. I have a fabulous hair stylist here. He swears I called back after our initial conversation to change my choice of hair color, hence the streaks of red. Luckily, I made time for him to darken my hair a little and soften the red, so it blended. Crisis averted. It was as if someone was trying to sabotage me." She shifted her look to Caroline, who was looking down into her soup pretending to not pay attention.

I thought it looked different, but it wasn't horrible. Well, it didn't look pretty. If this is part of the plan they set in place to help me win Ben back, I don't think it's working.

"Heather," Caroline finally looked up. "How is it you never came to marry or have children of your own?"

I could tell Ben felt uncomfortable about the question because he sent Caroline a stern look.

"I was just curious. You're very pretty, so I wondered why you've never been married or why you never had children," she continued loudly enough for all around to hear.

Ben shook his head in disapproval looking right at Caroline. Heather noticed.

"No, it's fine," Heather said, placing a hand on his shoulder. "I've been very busy going to school and working and, well, it just took me a long time to find that right person." She smiled at Ben.

"Did you want kids?" Caroline asked.

"Caroline!" Ben finally spoke up.

"Benny, really, it's okay." She patted his shoulder once again.

To hear her say 'Benny' made my stomach churn. I tried not to look up very much, I felt so uncomfortable and assumed the kids were trying to humiliate Heather. I wanted to just tell Ben how I felt. Why hadn't I been brave enough to do that?

"I didn't really want children, to be honest," Heather said

seriously.

"You never wanted kids? I didn't know that," Ben said in surprise.

"I thought you knew that," she said, removing her hand from his shoulder. "We've talked about this, haven't we, and really, what does it matter? I'm past that time in my life," she said, then took another bite of her salad.

Servers started to pass about the room taking eaten salad and soup dishes. They discreetly replaced them with the main course; roast duck with asparagus and au gratin potatoes. Soft music of stringed instruments played in the background.

"But what about grandkids?" Jared asked. "I want to have lots of babies with Mellie."

Mellie spit out her spoonful of soup and shot him a shocked smile. I guess Mellie's a lot more like me than I thought.

"I'm sure I will love my grandchildren," she smiled at Jared.

"You mean my grandkids," I blurted out. I can't believe I just said that.

"What's your problem, Madelyn?" Heather stood from her seat. I was so surprised by her reaction after she portrayed herself as being so well behaved and refined.

"Ladies, that's enough," Ben said sternly grabbing Heather by the shoulders and helping her to sit back down.

"This dinner is for Mellie and Jared," he continued. "Let's be respectful and put the focus on them."

Mellie shot me a wide-eyed smile and I flashed a concerned one back. I didn't like where this was going, but the kids seemed like they were enjoying it. The rest of the dinner was mostly silent. Mellie, Jared, and Caroline exchanged quiet conversation between them and other guests. Ben and Heather didn't talk for a while and then I heard whispers of arguing between them. Then came the toasts. All the guests who participated had such meaningful words to say. It was my turn. I stood confidently in my dashing dress.

"Mellie doesn't like me to say this, but I feel like I knew long before the two of them did, that they were meant to be together. Mellie is my joy and my world, and I don't think I could have hand-picked a better man to love her. Your Dad would be so proud of you, Mellie. I love you both."

I debated being done, but then hesitated for a moment. "Love is funny sometimes, you know. Sometimes it's easily found and recognized; sometimes it takes a while. It could be right there next to you and you don't even know it." I looked at Ben who had a blank expression on his face again. What was he thinking? I could usually tell, but not tonight. "To Mellie and Jared." I lifted my glass and drank.

"I would like to say something!" Heather jumped from her seat. "When I first met Caroline and Jared, they had already been dating and I knew they were meant to be together," she exclaimed.

"Mellie," I whispered. "You mean Mellie."

Todd started laughing loudly next to me. I'd almost forgotten he was there. He'd clearly had a few too many drinks already.

"Right, of course, I'm sorry; I meant Mellie." Heather laughed it off and so did a few other guests. Our table was not laughing. Ben was watching me.

Heather continued. "I think sometimes love can pass you by if you're too blind to see, and then we must forgive ourselves and move on if that happens. Mellie and Jared, I'm so glad that didn't happen to you. To the happy couple." She smirked back at me.

Now more than ever, I wanted to jump across this table and strangle her.

"I'm the father of the groom." Ben stood, tapping his fork against his glass. He looked at Jared. "I first want to say I know your mother Cassie would be so proud of who you and Caroline have become. You're the good man you are today because she was your mother. I take no credit in that. I was overjoyed to find out that our long-time neighbor and friend, Mellie, stole his heart away. To Jared and Mellie!" Glasses clinked, and everyone cheered.

Ben looked my way and paused, still standing. I wish I knew what he was thinking. I was teary eyed by now and gave him a soft smile. We've been through so much together and this was a special moment for both of us.

"To the mother of the bride," Ben continued. My heart started to race. He opened his mouth and then closed it. What did he want to say? Now Heather had the stoic look. He took a breath; "Mellie is amazing because you are amazing. Over the years I have watched you raise her and help to raise mine. Thank you for bringing joy back into my life and the lives of my children. I think your Luke and my Cassie would be so proud of you. Thank you. To Maddie!"

Glasses clinked along with multiple cheers. I covered my heart and smiled whole heartedly at Benny. He had my heart and he didn't even know it. I could see tears in his eyes, but he held them in very well. I looked over at the kids who were all crying and then began the hugs. For a moment I forgot all about Heather. In that instant she wasn't a part of our family. It was just the five of us, like it should be.

Heather stood and walked off throwing her napkin on her plate. Ben looked my way and then he got up and walked after her.

"I think it's working," Caroline whispered to us all.

"You three are terrible, and I love you for it," I smiled. "Now let me take over." They meant well, but humiliating her was not the way I wanted to do this.

Dancing came last, which I was usually happy to sit out. But this was my daughter's rehearsal dinner and I wanted to be a part of all of it.

"Wanna dance?" I asked looking over at a very drunk Todd.

"You know it, baby!"

"Oh, gross, Todd; your breath smells awful; how much did you drink?" I covered my nose, contemplating if this would be worth it.

"Not enough." He grabbed my hand and led me to the dance floor.

I tried to see if I could find Ben, but I didn't know if he and Heather had come back into the reception hall. I didn't have to encourage Todd at all, he just kept getting closer and closer. His hand slid down my dress from my back to my butt. I moved it back up.

"Too much, Todd," I said loudly and boldly still looking around for Ben.

Todd laughed and then slowly moved it back down.

"Cut it out," I said as I moved his hand back up. He had a tight grip around my waist and I was struggling to get out of his hold.

I suddenly felt my shoulder swing back. It was Ben. He grabbed me, pulling me back and pushing Todd hard in the process.

"She told you to cut it out!" He was angry.

"It's just friendly dancing, Ben. She liked it and she...."

Whack! Todd went flying across one of the beautifully decorated tables, shattered glass flying everywhere. The music stopped, and guests gasped and rushed to the commotion. The kids ran over and stood close by with wide eyes.

My sister Angela and her husband helped Todd up. I found myself frozen with my hands to my face between a drunk Todd and an angry Ben who was still clenching his fist and moving from me toward Todd. I had wanted to make him jealous, that's all. This had gotten way out of hand.

"You didn't have to hit him, Ben!" I yelled.

"Ben? My name is Ben now?" he questioned me, almost yelling.

I looked over at Heather. Her eyebrows couldn't be any higher.

"He's just a little drunk, that's all." I looked back at Ben.

"That's all!" Ben turned to face me.

"Maddie do you know why I made him leave that night?"

Even when his face burned red with anger he was still so handsome with his wavy dark hair and big brown eyes. And all I wanted to do was run my fingers along his face and kiss him.

"What are you talking about?" I asked.

"Over a year ago, I walked into your house and caught you kissing Todd, do you remember?" He was waving his hands as he spoke. He was always more physically animated when he was angry.

I heard a few gasps amongst the unsuspecting guests and family members.

"Of course, I remember, I also remember it being a one-sided kiss from Todd. What does that have to do with tonight?" I tried to say calmly and quickly as if no one would notice our yelled conversation.

"After you went to your room, he confessed his intentions." He looked back at Todd who was almost standing on his own and working his way back to us.

"What intentions?" Now I was looking at Todd.

Everyone was quiet and staring in wonder at Todd and then to me and then back to Ben. I kept wondering if Mellie was freaking out, but she looked just as intrigued as everyone else.

"He only came to your home with the idea of sleeping with you," Ben kept yelling, followed by a few more gasps and whispers.

"What? No!" I said unbelieving. "He just needed a place to stay while his house was being worked on."

"His house has never been renovated. He was just determined to sleep with you and then leave once he got what he wanted." He looked at Todd and then back to me, not yelling this time, but still bold.

"Is this true, Todd?" I looked at Todd with such disapproval.

"Look," he said with a crooked smile. "He's exaggerating—"

Whack! I looked down at my instantly red knuckles. That was me that just punched Todd in the face. He flew into another table, taking it and everything on it down with him once again. More gasps from the audience. The Pierre a Taj should really get some sturdier tables.

This time I don't think he was getting back up. I looked

at Ben; "and you kicked him out and told him never to come back." He was staring in amazement at the damage I made.

"Yes," he said, wide eyed and proud, looking back at me.

"Because you loved me?" I completely caught him off guard.

"Yes," he said, "wait, what?"

"And you still do?" I could see Heather out of the corner of my eye pursing her lips and furrowing her brow. She grabbed Ben's arm as if to remind me and him that he belonged to her.

"Maddie, it's too late," he said softly, his bold speaking became calm.

"No!" I yelled, catching many people, including Ben, by surprise. "It's not too late, Bennny!" I made sure to emphasize that for Heather's pleasure. "Me and you are here, now; we're alive. We couldn't control what happened to Cassie and Luke, but we can have a say in what happens to us now."

He was frozen with his mouth open. I looked around to find Mellie. She was smiling at me chewing on a piece of her hair in anticipation. The room was still silent around us, everyone watching us like we'd planned a post-dinner showing of some murder mystery with a love twist.

I continued to talk. "I love you, Benny, and it's the same way you love me. I have for a long time, but my heart just took forever to admit it. I want you, our lives together; I want to kiss you every day. I want to travel the world and get lost in weird places so that you have to find me."

I think I saw him smile a little bit. By this time, I had tears streaming down my face and so did Mellie and Caroline. My make-up was probably just as streaked as theirs. Jared still had his mouth wide open just watching.

But Benny said nothing, Heather still holding his arm tightly with her eyes wide open. I had to leave; I had to! I didn't know what else to do, but before I turned around to leave, I said one more thing; "Oh, by the way, Heather, Benny has seen me naked…and he *loved* it!"

I turned toward the door, hearing a few items dropping to the floor, followed by laughter, clapping, and cheering. I shut the giant door behind me feeling proud of myself for laying it all out on the table, including Todd. I knew if Benny turned me down now, I'd done everything I could to get him back.

I ran back to my room, nervous to what the aftermath of my actions might be. *Is it too late?* I thought to myself. Did I completely just humiliate myself and my family and Mellie? He knows now; no regrets.

Chapter Eleven

I waited for Ben to come, finally feeling the pain in my knuckles, but it was Mellie who came rushing through my door with Caroline.

"Mom, that was amazing!"

Caroline jumped in. "I can't believe you did that! That was the coolest thing I have ever seen; Dad punched that pervert and then you punched him, then you confessed your love to Dad, *finally*." Smiling at me with her hands to her chest. Then Caroline hugged me.

"It did feel good to hit that dirty perv," I laughed, "and to finally figure out my feelings for your dad."

Then someone started pounding on the door. It was Jared. He barreled through the door as soon as Mellie opened it. "That was the best rehearsal dinner I have ever been to in my entire life, the staff is down there right now trying to figure out what to do with a very drunk Todd." He let out a loud whoop of excitement.

Mellie smiled at me and mouthed, "I'm proud of you."

I smiled and mouthed back, "thank you."

"Now what?" I asked the kids. "Benny isn't here; he didn't come for me. I've only made a fool of myself and ruined your beautiful dinner."

Mellie grabbed my hand. "You did not ruin anything; everyone was talking about it. This was by far the best dinner party I have ever been to in my life. No one will ever forget it. I loved it."

"Plus, when we left the reception," Caroline chimed in, "Dad and Heather were in the hallway downstairs in deep discussion, maybe even arguing, probably about your naked body that he loves."

We all laughed, and I did a face palm.

"Mom, I had no idea you were so scandalous," Mellie said with a giggle.

"I knew she was; that's what I love about her." Caroline winked at me. "Oh, and the look on Heather's face was priceless. I will never forget that. Ever!"

"He will come, Mom; I know he will." Mellie smiled and grabbed my hand.

Jared left to go back downstairs and take care of the physical damage that had been made.

We stayed upstairs for a few hours talking and giggling and catching the girls up on my scandalous life, followed by their own surprising scandalous love stories.

Ben didn't come, nor did he text. Caroline went to her room to sleep while Mellie snuck out for a while with Jared on the night before their wedding day. I laid in bed, wondering if I would ever sleep. If I did, would I dream about me as the dinosaur eating the T-rex this time? I kept checking my phone. Nothing! I finally did fall asleep.

I woke up feeling refreshed and then quickly remembered the events of last night. I jumped out of bed, getting dressed this time. I ran and knocked on Benny's door.

"He checked out early this morning Ma'am." I looked over to see the cleaning maid about to go into Heather's room.

"Oh, do you happen to know why?" I asked.

"Him and the lady checked out together early this morning," she continued.

My heart sank. *No; No he chose her!*

I slowly stepped back into my room, looking around; everything was spinning. I turned and ran. I ran down the stairs, out of the hotel, past the waffle truck, past the Plaza and Tiffany's.

I kept running until I found myself back at the New York Library. Here is where I screwed it all up. Here is where I ended it all.

I wandered through the library for hours. Going down each aisle slowly and running my fingers across each book. Eventually I recognized the spot where I broke Ben's heart.

I stopped and grabbed the same book I was holding when he decided to confess his love to me. I sat down on the floor and opened it up. *A Tale of Two Cities; It was the best of times and the worst of times.* I shut the book and put my head down. I started to tear up at the irony, crying into my hands. After a while my tears started to slow.

"Ow!" *What just hit me?* I looked down and saw a red cinnamon bear lying next to me. I looked up to see Benny hiding behind a book shelf. "What are you doing here?" I said, quickly standing.

"I told you I would get you back." He came out from hiding and leaned against a tall shelf, folding his arms.

I laughed first, and then slightly smiled.

"Plus, didn't you say you always wanted me to find you in weird places?"

I smiled even bigger and started to tear up but tried to hold back.

"But what about Heather; you checked out with her early this morning?" I stopped smiling.

"I had a very long talk with her last night and dropped her off at the airport this morning." He stood up straight.

"Wow, I am so sorry, Benny."

"No; no, you're not." He laughed.

"Nope, I'm not." I smiled.

He laughed and slowly walked closer to me. "I think the last straw for her was something about me seeing you naked and loving it." My head fell in my hands in embarrassment.

He pulled my hands away from my face. "And I did, by the way."

I cringed and could feel my face burn.

"I'm sorry I said that, but I just hate her so much." I looked up at him locking his big brown eyes with mine.

"I know, she told me you did," he said, laughing.

"Well, I told her I hated her the night you proposed to her. She's been so mean to me, telling me that I can't be your friend or call you Benny—"

He interrupted my rant with a kiss. The most perfect of kisses; a second kiss. I had to grab his chest and neck to keep from falling. Once again, I could feel his stubble against my face as he kissed me ever so softly.

He held me close and I knew without a doubt that I loved

him. We kissed for quite some time, making up for all the time that we'd wasted not kissing.

"Excuse me; this is a library, not a park," a librarian sternly whispered to us.

We pulled away from each other, laughing and smiling. I picked up the cinnamon bear and threw it back at Benny. We walked down the steps of the library and leaned against one of the lion statues while he kissed me again and again.

"It's about time you figured it out, Maddie." He smiled and just hugged me.

"Wait," I pulled away from him. "The maid said that you checked out this morning, too; that makes no sense."

"Oh yes, about that, well…you see, Mellie and Jared will have their own room tonight, obviously, and I got Caroline her own room as well." His eyes were wandering a little bit during his explanation.

"That still doesn't make sense," I said, looking straight at him.

"I will be sleeping in your room tonight." He smiled confidently.

"Oh no; I have a pretty good right hook, Ben, just ask Todd." He grabbed my fist as I gestured to punch.

"I am not going to lose you ever again, Maddie. I want to marry you today in front of all our friends and family."

He got down on one knee.

"What, is this a joke, Benny?" I asked.

"Mellie and Caroline set it all up. We can be married before the kids, tonight, in a small ceremony, if you want, Maddie."

He brought out a ring; a solid gold band and put it on my finger.

"Please say yes, Maddie." He held his hand over mine.

"Oh, my goodness, is this really happening? Yes, my answer is yes."

He stood, picking me up in the air and kissing me again.

It only seemed right to get married in New York City I guess, seeing as this is where I found out I was in love for the second time.

The weddings were beautiful and perfect.

Ben had Todd escorted out of the hotel.

I sent Sam a text with Heather's phone number and Ben suggested "Endless Love" as our song to the DJ.

Ben had large amounts of cinnamon bears delivered to the hotel to be displayed on each of the tables.

I didn't think now would be a good time to tell him that I don't like cinnamon bears. For eating, anyway. Maybe I'll tell him tomorrow, after we wake up. Together.

The End
For Now

About the Author

Keri Brooks McWhorter is a sixth generation native of Chandler, Arizona. Her mother fed her love of books, and Keri's been writing all her life, starting with short stories in her childhood. She's a fourth-generation graduate of Chandler High school, and has a Bachelors in Psychology from Arizona State University. She served a mission for the LDS church in New York City, and met her husband while she was there. They have three children, a love of family, and an English Bulldog.

Connect with me online:

Website: www.electric-scroll.com
Email: k-mcwhorter@electric-scroll.com
Facebook: I Swear I'm a Writer

Made in the USA
San Bernardino, CA
27 June 2018